D0348966

Contents

Introduction

Sherluck Bones and Scotson are back for more fun. Come along and join the two famous detectives from Kennelwood as they once again solve mysteries, crimes, and puzzles. The quick brain of Sherluck Bones can solve a puzzle in two seconds flat, and his eagle eye can spot a clue a mile away. His good friend Scotson is always amazed at Sherluck's detecting skills.

The Sherluck Bones Mystery-Detective Book 6

by Jim and Mary Razzi

Pictures by Ted Enik

A Bantam Skylark Book®
Toronto / New York / London / Sydney

RL 3, 007–009

THE SHERLUCK BONES MYSTERY-DETECTIVE BOOK 6
A Bantam Skylark Book / April 1984

*Skylark Books is a registered trademark of Bantam Books, Inc.
Registered in U.S. Patent and Trademark Office and elsewhere.*

ISBN 0-553-15240-8

Published simultaneously in the United States and Canada

*Bantam Books are published by Bantam Books, Inc. Its trade-
mark, consisting of the words "Bantam Books" and the por-
trayal of a rooster, is Registered in U.S. Patent and Trademark
Office and in other countries. Marca Registrada. Bantam
Books, Inc., 666 Fifth Avenue, New York, New York 10103.*

PRINTED IN THE UNITED STATES OF AMERICA

CW   0 9 8 7 6 5 4 3 2 1

The Case of the Lying Workman

Pamela Poodle had invited Sherluck Bones and Scotson to come and see her new seaside cottage. The inside was a little dirty and run-down. Sherluck even had to break a giant spider web to get into the two back rooms. Pamela admitted that she had hired a workman to fix the place up.

At that moment, they heard a noise at the cottage entrance. It was Boris, the workman.

"Well, Boris," asked Pamela, "did you look the place over?"

"Indeed I did, from top to bottom," answered Boris. "And there's a lot of work to be done. It's going to cost a lot of money. Lucky for you I'm an expert!"

"Don't listen to him, Pamela," said Sherluck. "I don't think Boris is an expert anything—except an expert *liar!*"

Do you know why Bones said that?
Read ahead to see if you're right!

The Strange Footprints

Everyone in Kennelwood looked forward to the annual cake-baking contest. And Bones and Scotson were no exception.

"I say, Bones," said Scotson as they walked among the booths that displayed the cakes. "I wonder who's going to win this year? There are a lot of delicious-looking cakes here."

"Well," answered Bones, "the three favorites are Debbie Dachshund, Horatio Husky, and Bobby Bulldog."

Scotson nodded. He knew that Bones had named the three best bakers in Kennelwood. They started to discuss them as they walked along.

Debbie Dachshund was a sweet little thing who had just opened up a bake shop in Kennelwood. This was her first time in the contest, but everyone agreed that her cakes were among the best around.

On the other hand, Horatio Husky was big and gruff. He owned a shop near Debbie's and had been in business for years. Although his *cakes* were good, no one liked *him* very much.

He was a very nervous type and always in a hurry. In fact, just before the contest he had tripped over some sacks of flour and had broken his leg. He had to come to the contest in a cast and using a pair of crutches.

Bones and Scotson were talking about Horatio, when he came hobbling along on his crutches, looking grumpier than ever.

At that point, Scotson asked about Bobby Bulldog.

"Well," answered Bones, "Bobby doesn't own a bakery, but he *is* a very good baker. He just missed winning the contest by a hair last year."

Just then they heard a commotion from a booth nearby. The two detectives ran over to see what the trouble was.

When they got there, they found Debbie Dachshund in the middle of a small crowd. She was crying and talking to one of the judges. Bones and Scotson leaned forward to hear what she was saying.

". . . Yes, my cake was in a box in my bike basket," she told the judge. "I went to look for a friend and left my bike by a tree."

The judge nodded and said, "Go on."

"When I came back to get my cake out of the box," she continued, "I found that someone had eaten it!"

"All of it?" asked the judge.

"Well, almost," answered Debbie. "There was just this piece left." Tearfully she held up a small piece of cake.

"Why, that's a crime!" cried Scotson.

"Excuse me," said Bones, talking to Debbie. "Maybe we can help. Is your bike still where you left it?"

Debbie said that it was. Bones and Scotson told her to take them to the scene of the crime. When they got there, they saw footprints on the ground. It had rained a little that morning, and the ground was still soft.

"Are these your footprints, Debbie?" asked Bones, as he bent over to study them.

"Yes," answered Debbie.

Then Bones and Scotson noticed another set of footprints. The prints went right up to the bike and then away again.

"Hmm," said Scotson, looking at the prints. "These are the cake eater's prints all right, but they look strange."

Bones looked at them, too. "They do look a bit strange," he agreed.

Scotson scratched his head in puzzlement. "By george, Bones," he said. "Who or *what* could have made those prints?"

Bones straightened up with a little smile on his face.

"I think it's very clear who made those prints, Scotson," he said.

"Who?" asked Scotson and Debbie together.

Bones told them.

Do you know who made the strange footprints?

The solution is on the next page.

SOLUTION TO
The Strange Footprints

Bones told them that Horatio Husky had made the strange footprints. He could see that the small holes were made by crutches and the big hole was made by a cast.

When they caught up with Horatio, he admitted eating Debbie's cake. He wanted to be sure that she couldn't enter the contest. But he couldn't finish it all, so he had left that small piece.

There was still enough cake for Debbie to remain in the contest. The judges each tasted a little, and all agreed that it was delicious. Debbie won the contest after all!

The Stolen Skateboard

Bones and Scotson were walking to the general store to buy some birdseed for their friend Bonnie Beagle. Bonnie loved birds so much that she fed them outside her house every day.

"I guess Bonnie uses up a lot of birdseed," said Scotson.

"Yes," answered Bones. "She feeds the birds every day. And as a matter of fact," he continued, "always at the same time—ten o'clock in the morning."

"I know," said Scotson. "When Bonnie comes out of her house to feed the birds, you can be sure that it's ten o'clock. You can set your watch by it."

They were so busy talking that they didn't notice they were on a smooth path going down a hill. All of a sudden, a group of skateboarders came zigging and zagging around the two detectives.

"I say, Bones," said Scotson. "That looks like fun! I'd like to try it myself."

Just at that moment, a young skateboarder ran into Scotson. Scotson stumbled, and before he knew what was happening, he found himself on the skateboard, too. He went whizzing down the hill with the young skateboarder.

"Help! Help!" he cried as they went faster and faster.

At the bottom of the hill the road curved. The two of them zoomed around the curve at top speed, and Scotson went spinning off the skateboard. He landed with a plop on some soft grass at the side of the path.

Bones ran up to him with a little smile on his face. He could see that his old friend wasn't hurt at all.

"Are you okay, old boy?" he asked as he helped Scotson get up. "I thought you did very well."

Scotson just sputtered and turned red as he brushed himself off.

In a little while, Scotson felt steady enough to start walking again. They had walked only a few feet when they saw an argument going on nearby. It was between Todd Terrier and Charlie Chow. Bones and Scotson decided to see what it was all about.

When they reached Todd and Charlie, Bones asked what the problem was. Todd told him that he suspected Charlie of stealing his new red skateboard.

"When did this happen?" asked Scotson.

"At exactly eleven o'clock this morning," Todd answered.

"How do you know the exact time?" asked Bones.

"Because I had gotten off my skateboard to ask someone the time," Todd replied, "and when I got back to where I left it, my skateboard was gone!"

"Hmm," said Bones. "Please go on."

Todd went on to say that he saw someone go around a curve on a red skateboard.

"The thief was far away," Todd continued, "but it sure looked like Charlie on my skateboard!"

"Ha!" Charlie said with a smirk. "That's what I've been trying to tell you. It wasn't *me*. I was nowhere near this place at eleven o'clock."

"Oh?" asked Bones. "And where were you?"

"As a matter of fact," answered Charlie, "I was all the way over on the other side of town."

"Did anyone see you there?" asked Bones.

"Sure," Charlie replied. "It just so happens I was passing Bonnie Beagle's house at that time. She was just coming out to feed some dumb old birds. We know each other, so I gave her a little wave and she waved back."

Bones opened his mouth to speak, when Scotson suddenly said, "Hold on there! That excuse is no good at all!"

Bones gave a little nod.

"Oh, yeah?" Charlie sneered. "Why not?"

Why did Scotson say that Charlie's excuse was no good?

The solution is on the next page.

SOLUTION TO
The Stolen Skateboard

Scotson remembered that Bonnie always fed the birds at *ten o'clock* in the morning. Earlier that day, Bones and Scotson even joked that "You can set your watch by it."

When Charlie said that he was passing Bonnie Beagle's house at eleven o'clock and that she was feeding some birds, Scotson knew that Charlie had been there but at *ten o'clock*, not eleven o'clock as he claimed.

When caught in his lie, Charlie confessed that he did steal Todd's skateboard.

Bones and Scotson made Charlie apologize to Todd and bring back the stolen skateboard.

The Dishonest Workman

Pamela Poodle had just rented a small cottage by the seashore for a summer vacation. She was very excited, and she visited Bones and Scotson to tell them about it.

"The owner rented the cottage to me for a very small amount of money," Pamela told them. "All that I have to do is pay for the repairs. A workman by the name of Boris is looking the place over right now. He will let me know what has to be fixed."

Pamela went on to ask Bones and Scotson to come with her to the cottage to give her some advice. The two detectives agreed.

When they arrived, they looked all over for Boris, but they couldn't find him anywhere.

"He probably went over to his workshop to get some tools," said Pamela.

Bones nodded as the three of them went into the cottage. It was very small and had just one entrance. The first room they entered was a little parlor. It was dusty and dirty, but apart from that, it seemed to be in pretty good shape.

There was a doorway leading to two other rooms. It had an old spider web across it from top to bottom. Bones broke the web to get into the other rooms. Pamela and Scotson followed close behind Bones. The other two rooms were also dusty and dirty but otherwise looked all right, too.

"Well," said Bones, "with a little paint and a hammer and some nails, you could make this place look beautiful."

At that moment, they heard a noise at the cottage entrance. It was Boris. He came into the room rubbing his eyes and yawning.

"Well, Boris," asked Pamela, "did you look the place over?"

"Indeed I did," answered Boris. "And there's a lot of work to be done!"

"Oh?" said Scotson.

"Yes," said Boris, taking out a pencil and pad. "I'm an expert at this, you know."

Pamela and Scotson nodded.

"Now, let me see," said Boris. "The ceiling in the parlor has to be fixed. It's falling to pieces."

Pamela and Scotson nodded again.

"And these two rooms here are in terrible shape," continued Boris as he looked around.

"Really?" said Bones. "They seem all right to me."

"Well, that's because you're not an expert," said Boris smugly. Just before you got here, I went over these rooms inch by inch. And let me tell you, there's a lot of work to be done!"

"How much will it cost?" asked Pamela with a worried look.

"A lot of money," answered Boris, as he added up sums on his pad.

"Oh, dear." Pamela sighed. "Are you sure about all this? The owner told me that there wasn't much to be done."

"Well, that's because he's not an expert," said Boris with a smirk.

"Oh, dear." Pamela sighed again. "I guess this cottage is going to be expensive to fix up. After all, Boris is an expert, and he does know about these things."

"Don't worry, Pamela," said Bones calmly. "I don't think Boris is an expert anything—except an expert *liar!*"

"Why, Bones," cried Scotson. "What do you mean?"

"I mean," answered Bones, "that Boris was never even in these rooms. And he certainly never went over them inch by inch."

"But how do you know that?" asked Pamela.

How did Bones know that Boris hadn't been in the other two rooms?

The solution is on the next page.

SOLUTION TO
The Dishonest Workman

Bones reminded them that there had been an old spider web across the doorway to the other two rooms. In fact, he had had to break the web so they could get in.

If Boris had been in the rooms "just before," as he said, the spider web would have already been broken.

When caught in his lie, Boris admitted that he had taken a nap instead of looking at the cottage. Pamela fired him on the spot and told him that he was lazy as well as dishonest.

The Phony Explorer

Bones and Scotson belonged to the Kennel-wood Explorers Club, which met every month. This month, some new members were going to be voted in. To become a member, you had to have traveled to someplace interesting. Since Bones and Scotson had been to many different places, they were among the very first members of the club.

Even though it was a rainy evening, the two friends made their way to the monthly meeting. When they got to the club, they were met at the door by the club's president, Sir Edward Elkhound.

"Ah, Bones and Scotson," he said happily. "How nice to see you again."

Bones and Scotson told Sir Edward that it was nice to see him again, too.

"We have quite a few fellows who want to join our club," said Sir Edward as he brought them into the big parlor where the meeting would take place.

"Indeed," said Bones. "Do I know any of them?"

"Well, as a matter of fact, there's one fellow who says he's a good friend of yours. His name is Denny Dalmatian."

"Hmm," said Bones. "I'm afraid Denny is up to his old tricks. He isn't a good friend of *mine*. I don't even like him very much."

Bones went on to say that Denny was always bragging and trying to show off about the things he knew or the places he'd been.

"The only thing that I know Denny does well is photography," Bones added.

"Really?" asked Scotson. "What kind of photography?"

"All kinds," answered Bones. "He has quite a collection of camera gadgets."

Scotson nodded.

Just at that moment, the meeting was called
to order. Sir Edward announced that the first
thing to do was to vote in the new members. At
that, Denny Dalmatian came forward, and the
members asked him to tell about an interesting place he had visited. Denny told them that
he had been in a jungle where there were lots
of wild animals, strange plants, and myste-
rious statues. While he was talking, he held up
a photograph.

"I even had a picture of myself taken there,"
he said. With that, he passed the photo around
for all to see.

The photo showed Denny on a grassy hill with a jungle in the background. It looked like a hot place because the sun was burning brightly in the sky.

All the members were impressed. They agreed that Denny was indeed worthy of becoming a member. All except Bones, that is. He was still studying the photo. Then he noticed something very wrong. He realized that it was a trick photo and Denny hadn't really visited that place.

"Stop the vote!" shouted Bones. "This man is as much a fake as his photo."

All the members started to talk at once and asked Bones how he knew the picture was a fake. Bones told them.

How did Bones know that Denny had used trick photography?

The solution is on the next page.

SOLUTION TO
The Phony Explorer

When Bones looked at the photo, he noticed that Denny's shadow was in the wrong place according to where the sun was. That's when he realized that it was a trick photo. Denny must have put the jungle background onto a photo of himself on a lawn.

When Denny realized that he had been caught in a lie, he confessed that the photo was a fake. Needless to say, he wasn't allowed to be a member of the Explorers Club.

The Skiing Thief

It was a bright winter day, and Bones and Scotson were out skiing. It had just stopped snowing, and everything looked sparkling clean and white.

The two old friends had just come out of the ski lodge at the top of the mountain, and were standing at the top of a long, steep hill.

"I say, Scotson," said Bones. "Isn't skiing fun?"

"It—it sure is," stuttered Scotson, who was nervously looking down the hill. He wasn't as good a skier as Bones, and he was a little scared about going down that hill.

He was just about to suggest that Bones go without him, when his skis slid on a patch of ice. Before he knew what was happening, he was speeding down the slope.

"Say, wait for me!" yelled Bones behind him.

But Scotson couldn't hear a thing. He was too busy being scared to death.

Down the hill he went, faster and faster. He was waving his arms and twisting his body. He looked as if he were doing a dance! Then, all of a sudden, he found himself at the bottom. He slid to a stop.

Scotson stood there, huffing and puffing, as Bones came up beside him.

"I say, Scotson," he said. "That was the best display of trick skiing I've ever seen."

Scotson just looked at him with his mouth open as Bones patted him on the back. At that moment, they heard a voice behind them.

"Sherluck Bones, I need your help!" the voice said.

They turned around to see that it was Frankie Foxhound, the owner of the ski lodge at the top of the mountain. Bones and Scotson asked him what was wrong. Frankie told them that someone had just stolen the prize for the skiing contest that afternoon.

"It's a silver trophy, and it's worth a lot of money," Frankie said.

"Did anyone see the thief?" asked Bones.

"Yes," answered Frankie, "but he was on skis and wearing a ski mask, so we don't know who he is."

"Hmm," said Bones. "Did you see which way he went?"

Frankie pointed toward another trail. "He skied that way," he answered. "But he was going so fast, we couldn't follow him."

"I see," said Bones. Then he turned to Scotson and said, "Come on, old boy, let's see what we can find out."

And with that, the two detectives went skiing down the trail.

After a while, they saw a little cabin right off the trail. Smoke was curling up out of the chimney. There were a lot of tracks crisscrossing each other right by the entrance. It was hard to tell if anyone had just stopped there or not.

But Bones had a hunch.

"Let's see who's in that cabin, Scotson," he said.

They skied up to it and took off their skis. As they did, Bones noticed an old sled, a wooden barrel, and a small wooden box outside the cabin. They were all covered with snow from the recent snowfall. Lying on top of the box was a pair of skis. They were black and shiny and looked new.

While Bones continued to look at these things, Scotson knocked at the cabin door. In a few seconds the door was opened by none other than Chuck Chihuahua. Bones and Scotson both knew him. He was always up to some mischief and had been caught while doing dishonest things once or twice before.

When Chuck saw the two detectives, he snapped. "Oh, it's you two. What do you want?"

Bones came right to the point. "Someone has just stolen a silver trophy from Frankie Foxhound's ski lodge. Did you have anything to do with it?" he asked.

Chuck looked offended. "Me?" he said. "Of course not. As a matter of fact, I've been sleeping until just now."

Chuck went on to say that he had been in the cabin when it had started to snow. He had decided to take a nap until the snow stopped.

"And you haven't left the cabin to ski since the snow stopped?" asked Bones.

"That's right," answered Chuck smugly. "In fact, I haven't even been outside the cabin since it stopped snowing. I told you, I was taking a nap."

"Hmm," said Bones. "Just one more question—are those your skis on the box out there?"

"Of course they're my skis," answered Chuck. "So what?"

"So plenty," answered Bones. "It means that you have been out skiing since it stopped snowing."

"Oh, yeah?" sneered Chuck. "And how do you know that?"

How did Bones know that Chuck had been out skiing since it had stopped snowing?

The solution is on the next page.

SOLUTION TO
The Skiing Thief

When Bones was looking at the things outside the cabin, he noticed that everything was covered by the recent snowfall—everything except Chuck's *skis*! (Remember, they were "black and shiny. . . .")

He then knew that since the skis were *not* covered with snow, they must have been used *after* it had snowed.

Who Stole the Monkey?

Bones and Scotson were strolling through the park on their way to the zoo. Scotson seemed a little sad that day, and Bones asked him why.

"It's the weather." He sighed. "The whole sky is cloudy. It makes me feel gloomy."

Bones agreed that it was a dreary day.

"Why, the sun hasn't been out once all day," Scotson continued.

Just as Bones was about to agree again, they arrived at the entrance to the zoo.

"Here we are, old boy," said Bones. "Cheer up, maybe the animals will make you feel better."

Scotson nodded and began to perk up as they entered the zoo. He *was* very interested in animals. He perked up a bit more as they started to walk around.

"You know, Bones," he said with pride. "I know quite a lot about the animal kingdom."

"Really?" said Bones as they stopped by a small cage.

"Yes," said Scotson as they both peered in the cage. The cage seemed to be empty except for a small wooden box in the corner.

"Hmm," said Bones. "The animal must be inside that box. Let's see what it is." He looked up at a sign on the cage. It read: GOPHERUS POLYPHEMUS.

"Aha," said Scotson. "It's a gopher, of course."

"Hmm," Bones replied.

At that moment, the animal crawled out of its box. It was a turtle!

Scotson turned red and scratched his head.

"Must be a mistake," he said.

Just then a zoo keeper, Benny Beagle, came by.

"I say," said Scotson. "Where's the *Gopherus polyphemus*?"

"You're looking at it," answered Benny. "That's the proper name for that kind of turtle."

"Oh," said Scotson as he turned another shade of red.

Benny was about to say more when Clem Collie, another zoo keeper, came running up. Bones and Scotson were surprised to see him working there. They knew Clem was lazy. Bones suspected that he was also dishonest.

Clem ran right up to Benny. "You'd better come quick," he cried. "A monkey has just been stolen from the monkey house!"

Benny left with Clem right away. Bones and Scotson decided to go along, just in case they needed help. On the way, Clem told them what had happened. He said that he was in the back of the monkey house, feeding some monkeys, when all of a sudden he heard a noise at the entrance. He ran to see what it was.

"When I got to the front," he continued, "I saw an open cage. The monkey that was in it was gone!"

"What did you do then?" asked Benny.

"Well," answered Clem, "naturally I ran outside to see if I could catch the thief."

"Naturally," murmured Scotson.

"And did you?" asked Benny breathlessly.

Clem shook his head. "When I ran out, it was too late. I saw the thief's shadow on the ground as he turned the corner of a building. But when I got up to the corner and looked around, there was no one in sight."

"Now, now," said Scotson. "Don't feel too bad, you did all you could."

"Wait a minute, Scotson," said Bones. "I think Clem did more than that. I think Clem had something to do with the theft of that monkey!"

"But, Bones," sputtered Scotson, "what makes you say that?"

"Because there is one big mistake in Clem's story," answered Bones.

"What is it?" asked Benny and Scotson at the same time.

Do you know the mistake in Clem's story?

The solution is on the next page.

SOLUTION TO
Who Stole the Monkey?

As Bones and Scotson knew, the sun hadn't been out once that day. So when Clem said, ". . . I saw the thief's *shadow* on the ground," Bones knew that was impossible. You can't see a shadow without the sun!

When Clem saw that Bones was too smart for him, he gave up. He confessed that he had stolen the monkey earlier in the day and then made up the story to cover his crime.

ABOUT THE AUTHOR

JIM RAZZI is the bestselling author of numerous game, puzzle, and story books, including the Slimy's Book of Fun and Games series, and *The Genie in the Bottle* and *Dragons!*, in the Bantam Skylark Choose Your Own Adventure series. Well over two and a half million copies of his books have been sold in the United States, Great Britain, and Canada. One, *The Star Trek Puzzle Manual,* was on the New York Times bestseller list for a number of weeks. His book *Don't Open This Box!* was picked as one of the "Books of the Year" by the Child Study Association.

ABOUT THE ILLUSTRATOR

TED ENIK is a playwright, set designer, magazine artist, and cartoonist as well as a children's book illustrator. He has illustrated *Bob Fulton's Terrific Time Machine,* by Jerome Beatty, Jr.; the Slimy's Book of Fun and Games series, by Jim Razzi; *The Creature from Miller's Pond,* a Skylark Choose Your Own Adventure book; and *The Curse of Batterslea Hall,* a Choose Your Own Adventure book, all published by Bantam Books. Mr. Enik lives in New York City.

Here are more of the "kid-pleasing" paperbacks that everyone loves.